T0148302

Witness to a Massacre

Witness to a Massacre

Diana Pasqua

iUniverse, Inc.
New York   Bloomington

iUniverse books may be ordered through booksellers or by contacting:

iUniverse
1663 Liberty Drive
Bloomington, IN 47403
www.iuniverse.com
1-800-Authors (1-800-288-4677)

Because of the dynamic nature of the Internet, any Web addresses or
links contained in this book may have changed since publication and may
no longer be valid. The views expressed in this work are solely those of
the author and do not necessarily reflect the views of the publisher, and
the publisher hereby disclaims any responsibility for them.

ISBN: 978-1-4401-5468-3 (sc)
ISBN: 978-1-4401-5469-0 (ebook)

Printed in the United States of America

iUniverse rev. date: 07/6/2009

Chapter One

Mary's mother, Vera, who was born in Kentucky, came from a poor home. Vera saw no way out except to get married at a young age to escape the life she was in. She and her husband moved to California. Mary's mother was a rough lady who beat her if she didn't do all the work in her house. Her dad was hardly ever home; he would be considered a rolling stone. At times, he would show up to see both of them, but he always had an excuse to leave. He never supported them, and they lived off welfare. Mary was dressed in secondhand clothing donated by neighbors.

Vera knew a childless couple who had wanted Mary since the day she was born. The couple had moved to California and had a successful business. One day, Vera went to the hospital because she did not feel well. They discovered she had a tumor in her brain. She had thought things out for Mary's future and had decided that if the day came when she would not be around anymore, she would have the California couple adopt

Mary. Vera spoke with them, and it was agreed. She also decided not to be so rough on Mary.

Things changed considerably at the house, and Vera and Mary actually became friends. They baked cakes and cookies together and had lunches by the beach in the summer. She realized that Mary was a sweet child and a smart one. Mary enjoyed her mother's company when she was sweet to her.

Mary's dad, Bob, was a drunk and a womanizer, and he beat Vera when he visited. He also got drunk and verbally abused Mary. When he would get over his drunken spree, he would apologize to Mary. She was too afraid to answer him, so she would say things like "that's okay" and "I know you didn't mean it, so forget it," but inside, she knew he was mean. He was a handyman who traveled from house to house. Rumor had it that he was wanted by the police for robbing the elderly. Once he set foot in their homes, he would evaluate what they had. He had an eye for antiques and helped himself to whatever he wanted. He was very lucky that the police never got him, and that is why he kept on moving around. The people said he never finished a job. He would charge one hundred dollars a day and would start another project. When he would go back to the original job he had started, he would charge all over again. He was just a petty crook, and Mary knew it was just a matter of time before the police would catch up to him and he would be sent to jail, where he belonged.

He was born and raised in Kentucky. His parents dealt in whiskey made at home. The police always were arresting the father. Bob was beaten at a young age, and he rebelled. He left home at fifteen years old. He joined with an underhanded mob. They committed crimes ranging from robbery to murder. He got quite an education at a young age. He served some time for robbing a store, but he was not sixteen then, so they did not give him a long time in jail. He met all kinds of men while in jail. They traded addresses, and when he got home, he hooked up with them. They opened up a pool hall and did a lot of things there, like hustling. They also kept a lot of stolen goods in the rear of the pool hall.

The police got a phone call one day about the things that were going on in this pool hall and arrested all the people connected with the crimes. One more time, he went to jail, and this time, he was of age to do hard time. When he got out, he was twenty-three years old. He met Vera at a dance hall. She was quite a good-looking girl. He asked her to dance, and after that, he took her home. He had a car in those days and dressed very well. When she asked him what he did, he said he owned a florist shop. She was quite impressed, thinking he was a legitimate man and quite handsome at that. She asked if he was married, and he said, "No way; I like to travel light." She didn't like that response and made up her mind right there that she was going to change that.

They dated a while, and she found out she was pregnant. She didn't tell him in fear he would leave. She went to a woman that took care of things like that, but then Vera got cold feet and changed her mind. She decided to tell Bob. He did not like the news. They were at a restaurant, and he told her to get rid of it. She said she couldn't because the baby was three months old already and that would be murder. "Well," he said, "what do you want to do?" She suggested they get married. She was fifteen, but he thought she was older. When she told him her age, he knew he could go away for rape, so he agreed to marry her. He explained that he would hardly be around because his business took him from town to town.

She asked, "And what might that be? You told me you owned a florist shop."

He said, "I do, but I travel too. I do construction on the side. There are times when business is low, so I do jobs from house to house. I might not be around when you need me."

"Well," she replied, "I will have to deal with that." He asked why. She said, "Because I love you."

He said, "No one ever loved me. I guess we're going to be married, but I warn you now, I'm not an easy guy to be around at times."

She said, "I'll deal with that, if you don't mind."

They went to the next town. He bought her a white dress and shoes. He was dressed in a black suit. The justice of the peace married them, with his wife as a witness.

When they got back to Kentucky, they went to Vera's home to tell her mother. She did not like what she was hearing and said so. First thing she said was, "So you got pregnant to get out of here. So go on. You should grow up first, but you've already ruined your life. At least you were decent enough to get married. Wait until your dad hears this. There will be hell to pay. So I suggest you both leave here as fast as you can."

Vera said, "We thought we might stay with you for a while."

Her mother said, "Oh no you won't. I don't want to deal with your father when he hears what you did. You made your bed; now lie in it."

They had to leave and take a room in a motel. The neighborhood wasn't the greatest. The place was full of hookers. At night, the noise was never ending. Bob said, "I'm getting some money. Soon we're moving."

Vera was happy to hear that. She was afraid to be there, especially when he left for a while. She thought to herself, *It looks like you got yourself involved with a thief. You jumped from the frying pan into the fire.*

Months went by. They had Mary. When she was born, she looked like a doll. She was a good baby. By the time she was three years old, Vera hardly saw Bob and didn't complain; in fact, she was glad she never saw him because all he did was fight and complain and get drunk and verbally abuse them. When he was sober, he wasn't a bad guy, but he was hell to put up with when he was drunk. When he got drunk, little Mary would hide behind the door or stay under the table. She would hear him screaming at her mom. He scared the pants off her, so she would not go near him. At other times, he would hold her on his lap and kiss her and tell her she was his little girl and that he loved her. That's the part of him she loved. The other times, she lived in fear of him. He yelled at Vera and told her he would disappear if it weren't for Mary. He only came to see Mary and leave them money.

When he returned to the motel, he told her to pack up their things, that they were moving. At that time she had been eight months pregnant, and it had been hard for her to lift heavy packages or bend. He had helped her, and they had gotten into the car. Soon they had arrived at the house that he had rented. It was all furnished, and most of the things were old but usable. She had been delighted, especially that there was a room for the baby. They had unpacked and the next day went to buy a crib and baby clothes. He had suggested she enroll herself at a hospital nearby for the big day when the baby was due.

He had driven her to the hospital and left. When he came back, she was standing in front of the hospital and got into the car and told him she was hungry. He looked at her, started laughing, and said, "You mean I have to feed you too?" She smiled. She did not tell him she was in pain. "What did they say in the hospital?" he asked.

She said, "Well, they think the baby is due in two weeks, more or less."

He asked, "Are you okay?"

"No," she said and smiled, "my back hurts. I guess the baby is lying on my spine."

They arrived at the restaurant, and she went to the ladies' room. When she came back to the table, she saw all the food, sat down, and ate. She was starving. He told her, "You're eating for two people."

She smiled and said, "I can't wait until this is over. I'm uncomfortable."

He said, "Well, it looks like I'm going to be a dad. What do you think it is, a boy or girl?"

She said, "As long as it's healthy, who cares?" He agreed.

One day, Vera was in the hospital to get her checkup. When she got home, she saw three men sitting by her table in the kitchen. Bob opened the door and said, "We have company. They're here on business. Make yourself scarce. Go upstairs and lie down. I'll call you when they leave."

She took a look at one of the men. He had cold eyes, and he looked like a murderer. She went upstairs but kept the door open so she could hear what was going on. One of the men asked who she was. Bob said, "My wife." For a while, she could not hear anything that was said. They whispered a lot, and then a disagreement happened and they started screaming. She heard them say, "We need you on this score, so don't disappoint us."

Bob said, "Okay, you got it. Now leave. She has to come down to eat soon, and I don't want you guys here."

One of the men said, "What's the matter? We're not good enough?"

Bob said, "Don't be silly. She's innocent, and I want to keep her that way. In case something happens, she can't identify us."

"Good thinking," said one of the men. "We're going to call you tonight, so be ready."

"Yes, I'll be there; don't worry. Good-bye, and shut the door."

Bob went upstairs, and Vera made out that she was asleep. He woke her and told her to come down because he had food on the stove. She said, "Good. I'm hungry."

He said, "You're always hungry, so what's new?" He

started laughing. They sat down to eat, and he asked what they said at the hospital.

"Nothing new." She added, "Everything is going as it should."

"Great," he said. "By the way, I have to go out this evening, so keep yourself entertained until I get back. Okay?"

"Okay." she replied.

He said, "I like how you don't ask questions."

She said, "I guess if you wanted me to know, you would tell me, plus business bores me."

He started laughing. He said, "It pays for this house and clothes and the food, and that's all you have to know." She shook her head. She did not dare to get cute because he had a violent temper when he got angry, and she knew from her father not to push someone's buttons.

Chapter Two

It seemed as if Christmas was getting very close. Mary had to buy her mom something special, so she started babysitting weekends so she could earn a few dollars. Roy, a boy she knew from school, would join her, and they would do their homework together. Everyone was teasing them, calling them boyfriend and girlfriend. Mary was laughing, and so was Roy. "Let them say what they want. They won't believe we're only friends," said Mary.

Roy looked at her and said, "Well, you know, I like you very much, and I would like to think you like me too, Mary. So, what's wrong with saying we're a couple?"

She agreed. That was Mary's first boyfriend. They were together constantly for six years, and then Roy's parents moved away. That was a very sad day for both of them. The crowd gave him a going away party at the candy store. Everyone was too sad to listen to music. Even the store owner had tears in his eyes. Roy was well liked by everyone. He was a very nice boy.

Mary had told her mom she was going to Dottie's to do her homework. She went into her piggy bank and took a dollar she was saving for Christmas. But, at the time, she had no idea she was going to enjoy herself with the crowd from school. She said nothing to her mom. She didn't want her dad looking for her and embarrassing her in front of all her friends.

She and Dottie went to the candy store three times a week. They met up with all the guys and girls they went to school with. The word got around, and almost all the school was there, having a ball. This was fun compared to being at home listening to all those arguments.

It was getting close to Halloween, and this girl, Claire, was having a Halloween party. She invited everyone to her home. Her parents had a great place at the top of the hill. They owned a few stores and were wealthy. It was going to be a costume party, and a gift would be presented to the best costume—one for a girl and one for a guy.

Mary did not have a lot of money, so she did not think she would make it to the party. She told her mom about this party, and her mom said, "Let's make you something. What do you think you would like to go as?"

"I don't know yet. We have time for me to think about it. Thanks, Mom. You're a doll." She kissed her.

Vera said, "I have an idea. You want to hear it?"

"Sure," said Mary, "what is it?"

"I can dress you as an angel. I can make the wings from material I have in the closet and wire hangers.

How is that? We can get some fake flowers and make a wreath for your head."

"That sounds great, Mom. You're an angel for coming up with that idea."

They both laughed, and Vera said, "I'm no angel. I just want you to have fun with other children your age. I know it's no fun around here, and that's why you go out when your dad is here, and I can't blame you."

They went into the closet and pulled out all the white material. Vera was going to make sheer curtains for the bedroom but decided that her little girl was more important. She had no sewing machine, so she did everything by hand. She made the stitches very small so no one would notice. When she took all Mary's measurements and finished sewing the dress, she took out the wire hangers and attached them together with pliers. She made sure no sharp ends were sticking out so Mary would not get stuck. She draped the sheer material over the hangers and sewed it on, and she also taped them to make sure they were well attached.

Mary loved her costume and hugged her mom tight and kissed her, saying, "You're the best mom ever. Thanks, Mom."

Mary knew she had to get great marks in school to get away from home, so she studied hard each day and made sure she got good grades. She joined acting classes because she had always wanted to be an actress and a dancer and a singer.

Vera never told Bob about her ailment. She felt that he did not care and it was not his business. Anyway, she knew it was only a matter of time before he left, and frankly, she really looked forward to it. She did not want to depress Mary with the bad news until she had to, so she kept it to herself and rolled with the punches.

Mary and Dottie did their homework, and Mary had to go back home. She said, "I'll see you tomorrow after school, about three-thirty. I'm glad you found this fountain shop. It's time we had some fun. I'm so damned tired of hearing those two roar at each other. By now, I know every line, and frankly, it's boring." They both started laughing and hugged each other, and Mary went home.

When she got there, her parents were still at each other's throats. She went into her room and put on the radio so she did not have to hear it. She swore to herself that the day she would marry, it would not be to anyone near there. She wanted a nice man in her life, and it looked like everyone there came from the same background and thought this was a way of life. Dottie had said, "It's the same thing here; all they do is argue. I guess they're bored with each other. I disappear too. Usually I go and have a soda and stay for a few hours, listening to music at the candy store."

Mary had asked, "Where is this store? Can we go together?"

Dottie said, "Sure, we're going tomorrow. You can go too. There are a lot of guys and girls there. We have fun dancing and listening to music. Bring some money. We'll have a soda. If you don't buy something, the owner throws you out, so you have to spend money. We sit in the back in a booth and hang out for a while. We get away from all these boring grown-ups." They laughed and set a time.

Things did not get better through the years. By the time Mary was seven years old, she had gotten used to the arguments. It seemed as if her mother did not want to do anything about all the abuse. When Mary would see her father walk through the door, she would go to her room or go out to see her friends. He would ask, "Where do you think you're going?"

She would say, "To do my homework at Dottie's house. I'll be back soon and help with dinner."

He wouldn't say anything and would let her go. When she would arrive at Dottie's house, Dottie would say, "I see he's back, right?"

"Right. He's back, and I disappear. Who wants to hear it anymore? It never changes; it's the same thing over and over."

Mary's mom would get angry and yell right back. One day, he got up and hit her. That's when Mary started crying really loud. He turned around and yelled at Vera. "See what you made me do? Now my kid is afraid of me. Damn you."

Vera said, "Go back to that woman you live with. You think I don't know who she is? If you do, you're mistaken. I want to know if you beat her too."

He said, "When she needs it, I do. So what? All you women think you can get me trapped. Well, I have news for you. You can't. I'm a free soul and will be that way for the rest of my life."

One day, Mary got home to see her mom crying. She reached out to hug her and explained that her father wasn't coming home anymore. Mary was startled, but she did not lose control. She hugged her mom back and said, "We'll be okay. Don't cry." She hugged and kissed her mom.

Her mom was very sick, and the doctors said she did not have long to go. They were treating her for a brain tumor. She suffered tremendous headaches. That next week, Vera took Mary to the welfare office and applied for welfare. They were accepted, plus she had great coverage for her illness.

She lived for ten more years. By now, Mary was in her teens. She graduated with honors; she was very smart. Her mom sat in the audience, and her face hurt from smiling because she was so proud of her daughter. When Mary left with her, she took her to a restaurant, and they ate and hugged. What a wonderful day they had together.

When Mary thinks back, she smiles each time.

For extra money, Mary babysat on weekends for a neighbor, and she put her money away for when the day came she had to leave. Through the years, she saw her mom getting weaker. She knew the day was near. She would be alone a lot, but she said she didn't care because they lived by the beach.

One day when Mary got home from babysitting, she yelled out her mom's name and got no response. She went into the bedroom, and she saw her lying there, holding the Bible. A tear was still fresh on the side of her face.

Mary started yelling as she hugged her mom. Some neighbors heard the screams and came running in. The police were called. They took Vera's body out. Mary felt numb. The pain was so great. She just sat at the table, saying nothing. The neighbors decided to take her to their home overnight. She went without a fight. She could not sleep all night. She decided to go to her bed, where she was comfortable, so she left them a note. They were sleeping, and she did not want to disturb them. Once she got in her bed, she felt better. The tears kept flowing. She had known this would happen and had thought she was prepared, but no one ever can be.

The next morning, she called the couple her mother wanted her to live with. Alice and Kevin said they would come. They were there in seven hours. Both of them were crying. It was a very sad day. They helped Mary do the preparations for her mother's burial. They stayed two weeks and helped Mary pack her belongings.

It all happened so fast that Mary did not have time to think. All she knew was that they were very nice to take her in and told them as much. She explained that she did not want to live there for free, and being as they both worked, she would prepare meals and keep the place tidy. Alice kissed her cheek and told her she would have a beautiful view by the beach and hoped she would make some friends so she could have some fun. "We never had children, even though we wanted them," she said to Mary. "We're blessed to get you. We've known you since you were an infant, and we know you're a good girl. If we can do anything to soothe this pain you're carrying inside you, we will."

One day the phone rang. It was Mary's father. He had heard in town about what happened and knew the arrangement was to have Mary live with Alice and Kevin. She got on the phone and hardly spoke before hanging up. When Alice asked what he said, she replied, "Not much. He wants me to go live with him and his bride. I have no intentions of doing that. He ran off on my mom when she needed him the most, and I never will forgive that."

Alice hugged her and said, "You're home now. Soon that will be in the past. You have a new beginning with us. Do you have a dream?" she asked Mary.

"Yes, I do. I've always wanted to become an actress. I took acting classes in school. All my teachers said I was a natural, plus I sing and dance as well."

Alice said that Kevin knew some people in show business. He would get in touch with them as soon as she was ready. She could not believe her ears. This time, tears were streaming from joy. She liked these people and felt they liked her as well.

"I'm a lucky girl," she said. They all laughed and drank soda by the beach.

Kevin called his contacts, and they gave Mary an appointment to go for an audition. Alice said she would take her. Mary could not believe it. Alice bought her some great-looking clothes, as well as very expensive shoes. They went to the audition, and Mary got a bit nervous at first. Then she got up her courage and read from a script. They told her they would call her.

All the way home, Mary kept on asking Alice if she thought she had been any good. Alice said she was very believable and she thought she had been great.

When they got home, Kevin was in the kitchen having a cup of coffee. He asked, "How did it go?"

Alice said, "She was marvelous." Mary turned deep red. They all started laughing. "Hey, who knows? We might have a star here."

Kevin hugged her and said, "We'll do anything to help you, so don't worry your pretty little head over anything." He kissed her on the forehead.

She said that she didn't know how to thank them. He said, "No thanks necessary."

Chapter Three

Halloween night finally came. Everyone was excited to go to the party. Some made their costumes, and some bought them. They were all excited to be going because they knew they were going to have fun. There was going to be bobbing for apples and a big piñata with candy. There was also all the soda they could drink and cake, cookies, and candy galore. As they approached the house, it was all decorated with orange cobwebs and a few skeletons. They heard noises from a recording, and there was a coffin on the front lawn. They had gone all out, and the place looked fantastic. Roy took pictures so he could show his and Mary's folks. He also took her picture. She looked beautiful. His dad took pictures of them together. This was going to be some night. Mary said, "I'm so excited."

He said, "Me too."

His dad was laughing and said, "Have fun. I'll pick you both up later. Bye for now."

Mary said, "Bye, sir. Thank you."

They were entering the hallway and something

touched them. Mary started screaming. It was a veil of some sort that automatically touched whoever was entering. Everyone was laughing; it was very funny.

Mary had told Vera about Roy's dad picking her up to take them both to the party. Vera had laughed and said, "You have a boyfriend, and you didn't tell me?"

"No, Mom. He's my friend; that's all. He's in my class and a very nice boy; that's all. His dad is picking us up and dropping me off. What time can I stay until?"

"Whenever it ends. Will it be supervised?"

"Yes, Mom. The parents will be home all evening."

"That's good. Have fun and call me if you need me, okay?"

"Sure will, Mom, but I know I'll be okay. What will you be doing?"

"Well, I figure I'll have an exciting night watching TV." She laughed.

Mary laughed too. "There will be a lot of scary movies on tonight."

Vera said, "Well, in that case, I'll read a book. I want to sleep tonight."

Mary knew this boy from school. His name was Roy, and he liked Mary and had asked to take her to the Halloween party. She had said yes. He said, "I'll pick you up with my dad. He'll drive us, okay?"

"Sure," she said.

"What are you going as?" he asked.

She said, "An angel. My mom made the costume herself, and it looks great."

He said he was going as a vampire. They both were laughing. "We're going to make some couple on the dance floor—an angel and a vampire. Let's take pictures," he said. "I have my camera. We're going to have fun. What time do you have to get home?"

She said, "I don't know. Mom didn't tell me. I guess they'll decide when your dad gets there."

Mary's mom had to take her to buy white shoes because hers were shot. So Mary told him she had to go to the store and that she would talk to him later. Vera stopped off at the store and found fake flowers for the wreath for Mary's head. It was winter, so the summer shoes were on sale. Mary got lucky and found the right size. They had a small heel. That was Mary's first heeled shoe.

Roy's dad picked them up at eleven o'clock. He would have allowed them to stay later, but he had to get up early the next day to go to work. The kids told him all about the party. He was laughing out loud. He said, "Now I'm sorry I missed it. I thought for sure you would win first place, Mary. You're very pretty, and that is one heck of an outfit."

She replied, "Thank you, sir, but the winner deserved it. That was an original idea."

They got Mary home about eleven-thirty. Vera heard the car and opened the door. She saw her daughter beaming and knew she had had a great time. She thanked Roy's dad, and he said, "You know what? We should have gone. There were a lot of parents there, and they had a ball. By the way, you have a lovely little girl. She's very nice. I have to go to work, or I would have had them stay later."

Vera said, "Thank you for taking Mary. You have a lovely son too. Now, good night. It's getting cold here." She shut the door and waved good-bye.

The evening had been a blast, and the kids had had a great time. Everything was wonderful, and they had a lot of fun and had plenty of candy to take home with them if they wanted. The grown-ups who had attended had a great time as well, just watching all the children. The best prize for originality had been given to Doris. She had gone as the Hunchback of Notre Dame. She had a huge lump on her back and was painted all green and had walked hunched over. No one knew who she was until the contest took off. She had to say her name on stage. It was, by far, the best costume there. They could not decide who was the best-dressed guy there, so they decided it was a draw. A guy named Sam had gone as a pregnant rabbi. He was very funny. And his friend Johnny was dressed as a pregnant nun. They had to split the gift. It was a trophy, so they decided to take it for a month each and drew straws to see who got it first. Johnny won it for the first month.

Roy called the next day and said he was going to the store to have the pictures developed, and he wanted to know if Mary was interested in going. He was going to have a soda later.

Mary said, "Wait, I'll ask my mom."

Her mom said sure. He was there in five minutes, and they walked to the store. All the way, they talked about the party. They dropped off the film and then went to the candy store to meet up with the crowd. Everyone was all excited about Halloween night. That's all you heard all over the store. Everyone agreed that was the best party ever. That Monday, when everyone went back to school, the teachers all heard about Halloween night and were all glad to hear they had such a great time.

Roy's dad was offered a promotion, and they had to relocate to Texas. The company was going to furnish a home and two cars. This was his time to make more money and have a comfortable life. He didn't want to move but didn't have much choice, so he accepted. He was aware that his son was heartbroken but felt he had no choice. Mary and Roy called each other and wrote letters, but as life is, they had no choice but to go their own ways. Eventually Roy was eighteen, and he joined the paratroopers and fell in love and married a girl from Texas.

Chapter Four

Alice told Kevin that Mary was feeling insecure. Alice said, "That's what actors do at times if they are perfectionists. But from what I saw, they seemed very impressed, and I might add, so was I."

Mary sat very quietly, and Kevin said, "I bet you a quarter you got the part."

Mary started laughing and said, "If I get the part, I'll give you a dollar."

"So what's for dinner?" asked Kevin.

"We stopped off and got Chinese food," Alice replied.

"Great. Did you get spareribs?"

"A large one is in there. Let's eat; I'm starving." With that, Alice ended the conversation, and they sat down to eat.

After dinner, Mary stayed over to get some rest, rather than going back to her apartment. She was very tired. It had been a long day. She went to her room after she kissed everyone good night.

In the morning, she went to work at the costume

shop and found a nice woman asking for her. Mary said, "And who is asking for me?"

The woman said, "I work for the producer of the show you tried out for yesterday. He wants you to be at the same place next week, at nine sharp. Congratulations. You got hired."

Mary couldn't believe it. She called Alice right away. Alice got so excited she started yelling Kevin's name. When he got there and asked what was wrong, she handed him the phone, and Mary said, "I owe you a dollar. I was just hired."

Kevin said, "I told you so. See you later. Congratulations."

Mary told Alice about the producer, and Kevin had him checked out. It seemed he was producing a movie.

The producer told Mary he would be in Switzerland and when he got back Mary was to call him. Alice said, "When it's set up, I'll go with you."

Mary said, "Fine."

Two weeks went by, and Mary called the producer. His secretary answered and put him on. He remembered her immediately and told her to be there on Thursday if it was convenient for her.

Mary got a few jobs doing bit parts in movies. She was also a dancer in a few shows. Ten years went by, and she was a woman and wanted to go on her own.

Alice helped her look for a decent apartment that was affordable. Kevin helped her move in. She swore she would be by every weekend if possible, as Alice had tears in her eyes. Kevin told her not to hesitate to ask if she needed anything. She told him she would not.

They were wonderful to her, and she loved them very much.

She had a few jobs lined up and worked very hard, plus she attended parties to get some contacts. She had a job backstage sewing costumes, which brought in steady money. She took her career very seriously.

She loved her apartment. It was very cozy. She and her cat, Cuddles, were very happy. She would call Alice and Kevin every day so they would not worry. On days off, she would go to their home and cook great meals, and they would review what had happened all week. She really felt close to them, as if they were her parents. They were getting on in years, and she saw it.

On Christmas, she bought them a ticket to go to Rome. They had always wanted to go there but had never found the time. "Now you have to take the time. It's all paid for," Mary said, and she laughed. They were amazed at such a great gift. She said, "Don't worry. I'll take the cat and come here and look after the place. Just go and enjoy yourself. So start making arrangements. This is an open ticket, so you can make all your plans." They were so excited that they hugged her.

"What a lovely Christmas she gave us, Kevin."

"You deserve much more than this. You both have been wonderful to me from the day my mom died."

"This is a very expensive gift," Kevin said.

Mary said, "Yes, it is, and you're both worth every penny."

They handed her some gifts. She sat down and smiled when she opened one. She said, "How did you know I wanted this cashmere sweater?"

Alice said, "Each time we pass that store, I see you looking at it."

When Mary opened the next one, it was a silk scarf that matched the sweater. Then there was another box. It was slacks that matched both the sweater and the scarf.

Alice said, "There is a small box in that one."

Mary looked through the paper, and there was a small box. When she opened it, there were diamond earrings. She immediately put them on.

New Year's Eve arrived. Mary was invited to a party the crew had set up for the workers. She got there and saw many familiar faces from the screen, and they introduced themselves and started talking show biz talk. They asked if she was in the business, and she said yes. She told them she was just beginning and was taking small parts. One producer saw her and introduced himself. He asked if she was interested in a musical, and she said she danced and sang. He gave her a card and told her to call him after the holidays. He would be back in two weeks. He would be at his parents' home in Switzerland.

She went home, fed the cat, took a shower, and lay down to get some rest. She could not sleep, so she decided to take a ride through the hills, as she had done many times because it relaxed her. She was driving slowly, listening to music as usual, when a guy saw her and started to flirt. She got scared and went faster. He finally gave up and took off when he saw she was not interested.

She said to herself, "Now, Mary, that guy was cute. Why did you make him think you weren't interested?

Ah, well, such is life. I guess he wasn't that interested because he gave up right away." And she laughed.

She turned her car back toward her apartment and went home, saying, "Tomorrow is work, and I have to get some sleep." She parked the car, went upstairs, took the cat to bed, and slept until eight. She scurried through the apartment, trying not to be late. She got to work, and her boss said she had gotten a phone call. He had taken the number down, and she called. It was the producer, asking if they could see her Friday night at the same place. She said, "Of course. I'll be there. Thank you. See you Friday."

Friday came very fast. They had her read again. It wasn't as crowded as the last time.

When she finished, he said, "You're darn good. Would you be interested in this part?" She said she was and thanked him very much. "You'll have to be here early on Monday. We work all hours."

She said, "I'll be here," and thanked him again. They shook hands and off she went back to work. She had a girl covering for her, but the boss did not care. This girl was good at what she did, so he let Mary handle it.

She went to rehearsal and stayed there until the break of dawn. She felt exhausted, but she knew it was part of being an actress. She went straight home and went to bed. In bed, she called Alice, and Alice told her she was elated, and so was Kevin.

They yelled, "Break a leg. Now, get some sleep. You'll have a grueling schedule until they feel it's all done right. Good night. Sweet kisses. We love you."

"Love you both very much. Good night." She hung up the phone and went to sleep.

Mary was tired from doing so much work all day. She needed to clear her head and relax, and the way she always relaxed was driving at night with soft music by the mountains. She found them very relaxing.

She was taking her ride as usual. The brights of the car lights were on so she would not hit anything. It was very dark in the mountains. She made a right turn and saw three men standing over what seemed like a man's body. He lay in leaves, and the place was all red with blood. She said, "Oh, my God, look what I ran into."

They saw her as well, and two men jumped in their car and started to follow her fast. She panicked. She didn't know what to do. All she knew was she had better step on the gas until she hit the highway.

She was so scared that she totally forgot her cell phone sitting right there on her seat beside her. She drove as fast as she could until she saw bright lights. She sped faster until she reached the highway. As she looked down, she saw her cell phone.

She stopped the car, and she took pictures of the driver and the car plus the plate number. She then went to the other side and took pictures of the other man. They started yelling some things in Spanish. She then dialed 911 and got the operator and told her where she was and what she had seen earlier that evening. The operator told her the police were on their way. She asked Mary for her plate number and a description of her car. It seemed like hours until the police came. In actuality, it was five minutes. When the men saw the police, they started driving fast, but they yelled, "We have your plate number. Don't be too surprised if we see you again." As she was talking to an officer, two other officers jumped in their car and started chasing the men, but to no avail. They got away.

Mary went with the officers to the police station and gave them the cell phone with all the pictures. In less than an hour, the pictures were posted all over the Internet and television. The men were asked to turn themselves in to be questioned for murder.

Mary took the police to the place where she saw the body. The body had disappeared, but there were traces of blood all over the leaves. The police followed the blood past some trees. There was a house. They knocked at the door. There was no answer, so they looked inside. They saw five bodies lying all over the living room floor. With this, they broke in and went upstairs.

There was an elderly man nude in the tub. He had a bullet hole in his forehead, and the killers had cut his throat. They went into a room, and there was the body of another man. The killers had done the same to him. They ran to the basement, and there they saw an elderly lady with a bullet in her back, and the killers had sliced her throat as well. The place was all red with blood in every room. They went to the back of the house, where they found a little girl with two bullets in her chest. They heard moaning and picked her up and drove her to the nearest hospital. She was still alive. She kept asking for her mom.

"How can we tell her that her parents are dead?" one policeman said to the detective. They posted the story in the news, and it was all over the paper the next day but was broadcast on television in seconds.

The little girl was able to talk, but she spoke only

Spanish, so they got a nurse, and she told them what the girl said. Within an hour, there were two people looking for her. It turned out to be her uncle and his wife. They told the nurse there was someone missing; it was a newborn baby. When the police heard this, they returned to the house. They were searching for a baby. Then they heard some crying, so they ran to the basement where the elderly lady was lying face front.

She apparently was the grandmother. She had been hiding the baby so they wouldn't kill her too. The murderers must have found her kneeling, and the baby was well hidden under dirty laundry.

The police immediately took the baby to the hospital, and she was fine, just dirty and cold and hungry. The nurses fed her and changed her. Then the aunt went to identify her. "Si, this is the baby," she said, crying.

Mary was afraid to go to her home. A detective named Frank Bruno took her to a hotel under supervision. She had two policemen by her door all evening. She asked Frank to stay because she was shaking so badly that she was afraid to stay alone. They ordered dinner to the room and asked for a deck of cards to pass the time. She stayed up for three more hours, then fell asleep. All the while, Frank was in the room. He made her feel safe. He was lying on a couch across the room.

In the morning, they ate breakfast, and then he took her to her place to change clothes and feed her cat. They asked the landlady if anyone had been asking for her. She said no. He said, "If anyone comes here, you tell them she does not live here anymore."

She asked what was going on, and they told her. "Oh, my God," she screamed. "You must be a mess, you poor kid."

They went upstairs, and Mary showered. She was already late for work, so she called them and told them what was going on. They said if she wanted a week off, they had a cover for her. She said, "Yes, I need some time off. I'm very scared, and plus, I'm very tired. I had to sleep in a hotel all night and hardly slept."

Frank said, "Are you okay? If not, you can come to my house while I bathe and shower."

She asked what his wife would say. He laughed and said, "Oh, she divorced me a long time ago."

Mary said, "I'm sorry to hear that."

He smiled and said, "I'm okay. I just miss my daughter. She's a wonderful child."

They went to Frank's apartment. He felt embarrassed because the place was a mess. He explained that he was hardly ever home. "This job is very taxing, and I'm not a good housekeeper."

She laughed and said, "Most men aren't."

He laughed and said, "I guess you're right." He called his boss and told them Mary was with him and in no shape to be alone and that she had taken off a week from work. They okayed it for him to watch Mary until the case was closed.

They had the day all to themselves. He asked her if she felt hungry, and she said, "I could eat a horse."

"Well, this place doesn't serve horsemeat, but it has great Italian food. I've known the owners for a long time. I stop in frequently. Taste the homemade wine. I tell you, it's the greatest."

He got dressed in five minutes, and they drove to this little place. It looked like they were dining in Italy. The pictures were amazing. The decor wasn't very fancy, but the food was scrumptious. She said, "I guess they have a new customer now. I love all I ate."

Frank yelled, "Hey, Joe, come here. I want you to meet Mary."

Joe was a small man. He had an apron on. He came to the table, and Frank introduced them. "I'm very glad you like my food. Please come again." He asked the waiter to bring them some wine on him.

A television was on in the rear of the restaurant. There was an interruption, and the newsman said three men had been brought back from Mexico when they tried to cross over. They fit the description of the men who were being sought. The Mexican police had seen their descriptions and were all warned they were dangerous and armed. The police contacted California while they held them. The American police brought them back to the United States and were holding them without bail.

The men were brought to Frank's precinct to be interrogated. One guy was a young kid who did not want to do time in jail, so he started talking. He said the people were from Mexico. They could not find work since the fires had burned out most of the homes where they worked. The young man, who was married with two children, knew a guy named Tony. He was Mexican, too, but born In the United States. Tony dealt in drugs, and he needed a place to stash all his wares. They agreed on a price, and they stored them in the house where the massacre took place. No one but the men knew what was in the house. One day, Tony wanted to take some cocaine out to sell. The men could not find all the dope. Tony accused Fidel, the man who had taken him into his home, of robbing all the dope, and an argument broke out. Then Tony lost his temper and said, "I'll shoot your whole family if you do not come out with the satchel."

Fidel swore he knew nothing about what had happened to the drugs. He had been out looking for work all that day. They took the place apart, looking for the dope. Nothing. Then, Tony went upstairs. The old man was bathing. He shot him and cut his throat, and another dealer did the same downstairs with the women. They saw the little girl run to the back of the house in an old shed. They shot her twice in the chest and left her for dead. All the while, Fidel was screaming, "You killed my family."

"Yes, I did, and you're next, so get ready. I ask you once again, where is the stuff?"

Fidel ran outside of the house. The drug dealers followed him. They caught up to him and killed him as well. That's when Mary pulled over to make her turn, and they started to follow her. She might have died as well.

The police ran Tony's record. He was wanted in New York for dealing dope and for beating a man half to death. He had a record of doing drugs as well. This poor man got involved with this criminal without knowing who he was, just because he could not feed his family anymore. There was no work around. Everything was burned down from the fires all over the mountains in California. He had paid for it with his life, and so had his family. The young man went on to say that same day he had seen a guy they called Jose. He had been at the house and had left in a hurry. Jose was also known to do drugs and sell them.

"He must have heard about the stash," said Frank to his boss. "Let's get him, too. We ran his make. He is no angel. He has a record a mile long."

Mary went to Alice and Kevin. She was very scared, but they were there to protect her, plus no one knew of them. When they opened the door, they were in tears. "Where have you been? We went half nuts looking for you. Don't you answer your cell?"

Mary said, "The police have the cell phone. I'm so sorry." Frank walked up after parking the car, and Mary introduced him. "He's a detective assigned to watch me."

"We have a spare room for you, Frank. Sit down and have a drink. What will it be?" said Kevin.

"Just coffee. Thank you. It's been a long day."

Kevin said, "You look like you're about my size. I'll get you some things to sleep in and a pair of slippers. Make yourself comfortable for the time you're here."

"Well, this might take a week or two. We're investigating just how many people are involved in this gang."

Kevin said, "Stay as long as you want."

Mary said, "Frank, tomorrow I have to get the cat."

Kevin said, "I'll get her. You stay here with Frank. I don't want you there until this mess is over."

Frank said, "He's right. We have to stay out of

sight until my boss says otherwise. This mob means business."

Alice said to Kevin, "We're not opening the store tomorrow. I need to get myself in some kind of order. I'm a mess."

Kevin said, "Me too. My nerves feel like they're on fire."

Frank said, "What do you say, Mary? Should we take them to Joe's to eat tomorrow?"

She said, "That's a great idea. These two never get to go anywhere. All they do is work."

They finished their coffee and put on the eleven o'clock news. The story was the headline news. Everyone was looking for the rest of this mob. Frank said, "I bet, by tomorrow, we'll have all these suckers in jail."

Mary said, "I hope so. I have to go back to work soon."

He asked, "What kind of work do you do?"

She said, "I'm an actress and a singer and a dancer."

"Have you done much work?"

"Yes, I have. I danced in a Broadway show, plus I do bit parts in movies. I also work, sewing costumes backstage."

He said, "You keep yourself pretty busy. When do you date?"

Alice said, "You tell her, Frank. She should do more socializing. Are you married, Frank?"

"No, I'm divorced."

"Sorry to hear that," said Alice. "Do you date a lot?"

Frank replied, "No, I don't. I don't find the time."

"You're both alike, I see," she said and started laughing.

"I guess you're right, Alice, but someone has to pay the rent."

Frank got a phone call on his cell just then. It was his boss, informing him that they had taken in four more guys who were involved in stealing the dope. He added, "Thank goodness for the rats, huh?"

Frank said, "You bet. They'd rat out their mother to stay out of jail. We'll have this case closed real soon. We're dealing with a bunch of mutts. They're spilling out their guts as we speak."

Frank had the speaker on so everyone could hear it. Then he said good night to his boss. He said, "What did you think of that? Wasn't that fast? These junkies rat each other out right away. That's why they do drugs. They're weaklings to begin with. They get in situations and then spill out their guts."

Frank stayed a week at Alice and Kevin's house. They got to know him, and they liked him. They saw he liked Mary, and she liked him.

"What do you think, Alice?" said Kevin.

"Oh, yeah, this is the perfect match. They have a lot in common and get along very well. Cross your fingers, darling. It will be good to have him around. At least we'll know she'll be safe."

The media was having a great time with this story. It was in all the papers and the news on television. One broadcaster said they were looking for Mary to hear her side of the story.

Mary said, "I'm not going to be interviewed. I just

want this to be over soon so we can go back to being normal people."

Frank said, "Don't you worry your pretty little head about anything. They don't know what you look like or where to find you. I guess when you go to court, then they will mass around you, but I'll have a car waiting outside. We'll make a fast dash and get away."

"When do you think I have to appear in court, Frank?"

"I would say, when my boss is satisfied that he got the whole crew, then they will go before a judge for sentencing. I guess by next week."

"I'm scared, Frank."

"You have nothing to worry about. I'm watching you, and if anyone harmed you, I would kill the bastards."

"Gee, Frank, are you this way with all the people you guard?"

"No, I'm not, young lady. Only you."

"Why me?"

"Because you're one special lady, that's why. And I have feelings for you." She stopped in front of him, reached out, and kissed him. He grabbed her and kissed hard and long. They both had a lot of feelings for one another.

Alice kicked Kevin under the table and nodded at Frank and Mary. Kevin smiled and said, "I always knew you were a witch."

She laughed. "It's as obvious as the nose on your face that these two belong together."

Mary and Frank were together day and night, and Mary was falling in love with Frank. He went and brought her flowers and kissed her and said he loved her. "Once this mess is over, we're going to do some serious talking," he said. She nodded and winked. He smiled.

A week went by. Mary had to go back to work, but Frank sat near her all day to make sure she was okay. Her boss allowed it. He did not get in the way.

One night, Frank informed her that they had to appear in court on the fifteenth of that month. That's when the trial was to begin.

"How long does all this take, honey?"

"I don't know. It depends on how much they got on these guys. It shouldn't take long. They all informed on each other. I think it will take no more than a day, and the judge will sentence them and throw the key away."

Mary started feeling tense again. She wanted all this to be over. He put his arms around her and said, "Don't worry, honey. No one will hurt you as long as I'm alive."

She put her head on his shoulder and asked if he would be around the rest of her life. He said, "You bet. No one can take you from me. And I will go wherever you have to go."

She said, "Well, I was offered a job on Broadway."

He said, "In New York?"

She replied, "Yes, hon, but I refused it."

"Why, babe?"

"Well, I was thinking of us, and I couldn't leave you."

"Well, sweets, if it's very important to you, I would go with you. That's no problem. I can always get switched around."

"You would do that for me?" Mary was touched.

"There's not much I wouldn't do for you, my Mary. I love you."

"Well, I love you, too, and frankly speaking, I would be very happy to be your bride and have your kids."

Frank was surprised. "You're kidding?"

"No, I'm not."

They started planning the wedding that night. He knew a lot of places that had great halls. She started looking in magazines for a wedding gown. They told Alice and Kevin the next day, and they were delighted. Kevin brought out the wine and made a toast. He said, "May all your troubles be little ones. And may God bless you both." He reached out and hugged Frank and kissed Mary on the cheek.

Alice had tears in her eyes and said, "Our little girl grew up." She kissed her. "So, when's the wedding?"

"We figure we would like to get married on New Year's Eve."

"Great choice. That's a great day for fresh starts," said Alice.

The trial started. It took two weeks, and the judge threw the book at them. After the trial, the reporters were rushing at Mary. It was a mob scene. Frank had ordered a car and had her run to it quickly. He got in, too, and slammed the door. "Hit the gas, bro. They're running after the car." They sped as fast as they could in that traffic. Finally, they lost them. "See, it wasn't as bad as you thought. Now, was it?"

"No, Frank. That's because you took charge."

"Of course, I did. They are like a bunch of nuts

after the story. They would have made you a nervous wreck."

They went to Alice's house and picked up the cat. They went to Mary's house and picked up some clothes. He then told her he had made reservations in a hotel.

She smiled and said, "I thought this day would never come." She laughed, and so did he.

"It's over, hon. It's over. No more pressure from anyone anymore; I promise." He bent down and kissed her. They made love for hours, and she fell asleep in his arms as he kissed her forehead and looked at his love. Finally, he fell asleep too. When they woke, they were hungry, so they called in for food. They sat up in the bed and ate and kissed.

"I've been thinking, Mary."

She said, "What, hon?"

"I always pass this house in the suburbs. It's a great little house. It's big enough for a family. I would like for you to see it, if it's okay with you."

Mary was excited about his idea. "When do you want to go?"

"I figure next weekend. I'll call the real estate agents and have them show it to us."

"Fine, hon. I'm dying to see it."

"Wait. When you do, I promise you'll love it. I can just picture us and our kids living there. It's a great house and a quiet area." Frank was beaming.

"How many kids do you want, Frank?"

"I figure two is okay. How many do you want?"

"Two is good, Frank."

"Settled then. We're having two." He smiled. He

wanted to burst at the seams. He had gotten the girl he wanted. Soon he was going to make her his bride, and she was willing to move to the house he had dreamt of living in. *I have it all*, he thought as he smiled.

She said, "Why are you smiling like a Cheshire cat?"

He said, "Because God granted me you and everything looks swell."

They went to see the house that Saturday, and she loved it immediately. He loved it too. They signed a contract. He took out a checkbook and made a down payment. They got the keys and decided to go home and get some pillows and covers and make love in their brand new house.

New Year's was just three months away. She had the gown and shoes, and he was planning to rent a tux. The invitations were all sent out, and gifts were coming from well-wishing friends. One day, a strange package with no return address came to the house. It read Mary's name. She opened it up. It was full of money and a note wishing them both well, but it had no signature. Mary showed Frank this and could not imagine who would send ten thousand dollars to her in cash.

"How was it delivered?" Frank asked.

"By postman, hon."

"We can't have it traced. Anyone could have sent it. Obviously, you have a rich relative who wants no one to know his or her business. But I find that very strange."

"So do I, Frank. We can't send it back. It has no return address."

"Well, we'll keep it in the bank for a while. Then we'll use it if no one claims it in a year. How's that?"

"Well, we have no choice, do we?"

"But it's a hell of a gift."

Alice and Kevin were told about the package, and they didn't know what to make of it either. "Put it away, Mary," said Kevin. "You'll need it if you have kids."

New Year's was upon them. Mary was getting dressed with Alice's help. She made a lovely bride. Kevin was with Frank. They both were nervous as hell, so they went for a drink at the bar. When they got to the church, the place was packed with family and other people they knew. The music started playing, and Kevin gave away the bride. The preacher was talking forever, it seemed. Then Frank heard the words "Do you, Mary, take Frank to be your wedded husband?"

She replied, "Yes, I do."

"And do you, Frank, take Mary as your wife, to cherish and love?"

"Yes, I do."

"Well, you may kiss the bride. I pronounce you husband and wife." Frank helped her pull her veil up and kissed her smooth lips and whispered, "I love you."

She whispered, "I love you too." She kissed him back.

The photographers took pictures, and the women cried. As they left the church, rice was thrown at them for luck. All the guys he worked with were yelling, "Hey, buddy, good luck. Meet you at the hall. We're going to put a package on tonight."

Frank yelled back, "Sure. That's why we picked

New Year's Eve—so your wives can't holler." They all were laughing.

They got in the limousines and met at the catering hall. Mary and Frank were seated, and so were Alice and Kevin. The band was playing great tunes, and people were having a great time blowing horns for New Year's and celebrating their wedding at the same time. The wedding was a lot of fun. They danced and ate all night. Then Mary disappeared and changed her dress. She tossed her flowers, and a redhead who was on a date with one of Frank's buddies caught it. Frank yelled, "You're next, buddy."

He said, "No way," and everyone was laughing.

The time came for them to leave and go on a honeymoon. They ran off to the car and took off to the house to pick up the tickets for the plane. They went to Bermuda for a week. They loved the hotel and the weather. She kept repeating her last name, and he asked, "What are you doing?"

She said, "Practicing my name."

He was smiling. So was she. They chose great furniture for their home. Then one day, Mary was sick in the morning. About a year had gone by, and they had not been using protection. She knew automatically that she was pregnant with Frank's child. She went to see her doctor, and he said, "You, my dear, are with child."

She made a special dinner for them, lit candles, and set the table very nicely. When he got home, he asked if they were having guests. She said, "No, silly. Why do you ask?"

He said, "Pretty fancy for a weeknight, don't you think?"

She said, "Sit down, Frank. I have something to tell you." She told him she went to the doctor and she was pregnant. He stood up fast, grabbed her, and kissed her, and he did not know what to say. She said, "You look stunned. Are you okay?"

He replied, "Yes, I'm okay, but this kind of rocked my boat. When is the baby due?"

"In six months."

"Well, we have to decorate the baby's room and get furniture. Did he say if it's a boy or girl?"

"No, I didn't want to know. It's a surprise."

Frank said, "I bet it's a boy."

"And if it's a girl, then what?"

"Whatever the baby is, it's ours, and all I want is for the baby to be healthy."

She said, "Me, too." She hugged him. She put on soft music, and they ate.

The phone rang. It was Alice, and they gave her the good news. She was so excited that she started yelling, "Oh, boy. I'm going to be a grandma. Wait till Kevin hears this."

Mary and Alice were shopping for months for the baby. The room and all the clothes were ready for the addition to the family. One night, about three in the morning, Mary wasn't feeling very well, so she woke Frank up and told him she thought she was ready to go give birth to their child.

He helped put her in the car, and when he went to start it, he realized his keys were in the pocket of his pants, so he had to go inside to get them. He was so nervous that he did not say a word until it was all over six hours later.

The doctor went to him and said, "Congratulations. You're the father of a son."

Frank went to Mary's room, but she was fast asleep. He sat there, just staring at his wonderful wife. A nurse came in and asked if he wanted to see his new baby. He followed her and stood behind a window. "That one is yours," she said.

"I would have known him anywhere. He looks just like us." The baby was named Ethan, after Frank's dad.

Two years later, Mary gave birth to another son. He was named Kevin after his other granddad. Frank was a very proud dad. Before they knew it, the kids were in school, and Mary decided to get a part-time job. She was home before the boys came home. They liked to see her there so that she could give them food and drinks. She took a job in a real estate office. She picked her hours and days. She liked the people she worked with, and it got her out of the house for a few hours.

Mary was sitting at home, having a cup of tea. She was thinking about her life and how she was very lucky. She thought about Alice and Kevin and how they had turned her life around. She knew she was watched by angels; it started at a very young age, after her mom died.

The last time she heard from Roy, he had three children and was very happy. She had been different. She had wanted a career, so she had not committed to anyone until she met Frank. After her mom died, she had been taken in by Alice and Kevin. She was doing very well, except for that awful night when she was at the wrong place at the wrong time. Since then, she had had trouble sleeping. Each time she thought of that night, shivers crawled up and down her spine. *What an awful thing to happen to an entire family*, she thought. *They say out of any negative thing, some positive things happen*, she thought to herself while sitting at that table, drinking coffee. She certainly agreed with that. Who figured she would meet Frank, the man of her dreams, and would love him so much that she gave up her dream of becoming an actress?

She looked around at her lovely home and considered herself very lucky. Then her kids came in for a snack. She smiled and felt that she really knew what happiness was. Alice dropped in each day to have coffee, and then Kevin picked her up. *They are heaven to be around. There is nothing like loving or being loved*, Mary said to herself.

At the same time, she heard a car at the side of the house. She knew by the sound that it was Frank's car. He yelled, "Honey, I'm home." He kissed her on the cheek and asked what was for dinner.

She smiled and said, "I thought we were going out to eat tonight."

He looked at her and said, "You want to dine out? Then get dressed."

She laughed and said, "It's in the oven, silly. I'm teasing."

He looked her in the eyes and said, "You cannot mess with an old cop. I smelled it down the road." He laughed. "Hey, guess what I found?"

She said, "What?"

"They just opened a new store where they bake bread of all sorts. It's still hot."

"It smells great," she said. "Let's see." She stuck her hand in the bag, ran to the refrigerator to get the cream cheese, and ate a piece of bread. "Wow. This is good. Where's this store at?"

"Well, it's on my way home. I'll bring you there on my day off, so you can go yourself and select what you want. Wait until you see this place. He makes up any kind of bread you want, and the price is not bad."

Mary said, "Sounds great. We're coming up in the world. Soon we're going to be on the map."

"Now, now, Mary. Control yourself. I'd rather have it this way. If this neighborhood gets too congested, I don't think we would be as happy as we are.

"You're right, sweetie." She kissed him. He smiled, yelled for the kids, and they came running in with mud all over their shoes. She looked at the footprints and yelled, "Halt right where you are. Go by the door, and kick off those muddy shoes."

"You heard the sergeant," he told the kids and laughed.

"You clean it, then. It's all day."

"Okay, okay, I'll do it. Darn. See what you get when you get married?" He winked at the kids. They hugged their dad. She laughed. They were happy, and that's all she needed in this world.

One day, the postman gave Mary a package. She looked at the return label. It had her dad's name on it. She took it inside, sat down at the kitchen table, stared at the package a while, then decided to open it. She saw two letters, each written in different handwriting. She opened one and read. It was from her dad. He said he was an old man and felt he did not have that much time left in this world. That was why he was writing this letter. She felt the tears swelling in her throat as they welled in her eyes. She continued reading. She was trembling but kept on. He said he had loved her from the day he first saw her, but he had been a bum and knew he felt trapped by her mom. He told her not to think it had anything to do with her. He continued to say he was a drinker and when he got in that condition, he didn't remember for days what he said or did. He went on to say that if at any time he had hurt her, he was very sorry from the bottom of his heart. He realized that she had been a baby and did not know what it was like to have a child with someone whom you do not love, yet you love the child more than anyone can imagine. He wrote:

Mary, you are the sunshine of my life. You are the only decent thing I have ever done. Even though I do not deserve such a wonderful gift as you, God decided to warrant you to me. I want nothing more than happiness for you and your children. At times, I have passed by your home and seen them. They are just wonderful, and your husband seems to be a wonderful man. May God bless you all. In closing, I want you to remember me as a man that loved and cherished you. You're a very special lady. You deserve love and happiness. It's too bad that things turned out as they did. Your mom hid the fact that she was sick. Had I known all this, I would have made an effort to stay on your behalf. But maybe if I did, you would never have met this great guy that you married. So God had his own plan. I had Ella send you this. I believe she wrote you a letter as well. Those were her instructions upon my demise. May God bless you and your wonderful family. All my love, Dad."

She put the letter down, had a good cry, and then looked in the box. It was full of hundred dollar bills. *He apparently was putting money away for me all through these years without my knowledge.* She opened up the other letter. It was from the lady he called Ella. She went on to say that he had struck it rich, and this money had been set aside for her and her family. She left a telephone number and asked her to call her. By now, Mary was a mess from crying.

Frank walked in, looked at her face, and he screamed, "What's wrong, honey? Why are you crying?"

She said, "Look at this, honey. I can hardly believe it."

He stood next to her and read the letter. Then he read Ella's letter. Mary showed him what was in the box. He could hardly believe his eyes. They both were in shock. He pulled out all the money. There was close to a million dollars in one hundred dollar bills. He said, "We're set for life, and the kids can go to college. We can pay off our home. Travel. Do what and how we please."

Mary said, "Now you can retire, honey. She says there's a lot of stock in my name in her safe. I guess she wants to meet us. That's why she held the documents there instead of sending them with this money. Can you believe this? It's all like a dream—and a hell of a dream it is too."

They both laughed. "So when are we going to see this lady?" he asked.

"I have to call her back. I could not think straight. Put that money away. If the kids see it, the whole neighborhood will know we're loaded."

He scurried and put everything in their bedroom, and then the kids ran in to say hi.

"Mommy will be right with you. I have to make a phone call. Okay?"

"Sure, Mom. Do what you got to do." And they laughed.

She called Ella, and they spoke a while. She seemed like a very nice lady. Mary invited her to the house. She accepted, and they set up the visit for the next day at seven. Mary suggested she stay and have dinner. She said it would be her pleasure and could she bring something? Mary said, "Sure. Bring an appetite." They both laughed and said good-bye, and then Frank came out of the bedroom, kissed the kids hi, and kissed his love, Mary.

She told him she had invited Ella over for dinner tomorrow. He said, "Good. I'm taking the day off."

"And well deserved, too, honey. Take the week off. Pretty soon, you're going to go on a long, well-deserved vacation as soon as the kids have off for Christmas, which is very near."

He said, "Let's go out and celebrate this good luck."

She dressed the kids in something warm. He went into the bedroom, put all the money in a suitcase, and threw it in the trunk of the car. They all went out to a fancy restaurant. No one looked at prices. They just ate whatever they wanted. That was a strange feeling. They had lived on a budget for quite a long time.

They called the number in Ella's letter. She answered. Mary said she had just received the box and read the letters. "What happened to my dad?"

Ella said, "He's been dead three days now. He had lung cancer, and they couldn't save him."

"Where did all this money come from?" said Mary.

"He invested in some stock years ago. It kept growing. The man was worth a fortune overnight. He provided for me quite handsomely. We had gotten married after your mom's demise. He made me promise I would do this, plus I have stocks in your name in my safe. You're worth a fortune, young lady. That man loved you very much. It was unfortunate that he did not get along with your mom, but I had nothing to do with that. I met him years later in Vegas."

They made arrangements for Mary to go to where she was. She, in turn, said she lived very close to her at her father's insistence. "He would pass by every so often to see that you were okay."

Mary said, "This is too much for me right now. It doesn't sink in. I'll call you later, if you don't mind."

"Sure, take it easy," said Ella. "I can understand what you're going through. I'll be home all night. Talk to you later. Bye."

"Bye," said Mary.

When they got home, Mary called Alice and told her the news. She had to sit down and give Kevin the phone. She could not believe what she was listening to. Kevin said, "Can we meet this lady as well, Mary?"

"Sure. Be here for dinner. See you tomorrow."

"Good night, hon. This is the best news yet." Frank and Mary both were in shock.

Mary had all the food catered. She loved Italian food and thought that most other people loved it too. She would not settle for anything but the best, so she ordered fish and meat plus all the cheeses. She loved stuffed mushrooms, so she ordered a platter with all the trimmings. She wanted all the kinds of breads they had, plus the house wine. She loved red wine. She also ordered white wine, just in case someone wanted some, and a case of sodas for mixed drinks or for the children. When she finished, the bill came to about three hundred dollars. She told them she would pay cash when they delivered. They were known for the best kind of ravioli. She wanted two dozen. Then she called Ella, and she asked her if she could get there earlier than everyone else. That way, they could get acquainted and talk a while.

Ella said, "Sure. I live only a few minutes from your house. We have been here since a few months after you moved here. Your dad would pass by faithfully each day to see you and the children. He would check the house out. It shows if you have no money to fix it. He kept telling me you were all fine."

Mary was astounded that she had never noticed him passing by.

Ella said, "Have you ever noticed the mansion on the hill?"

Mary said, "It's some place. Why?"

"Well, we bought it. And it goes to you when I die.

We never had children, so I guess you're it, you lucky girl. Do you mind if I come now, Mary?"

"Not at all. Come on over. You sound like quite an interesting person. And I know I'll enjoy your company."

Ella was over at her house in about twenty minutes. Mary heard the doorbell, and the kids answered it. They yelled, "Hey, Mom. There's someone here to see you." When Ella saw Mary, she hugged her. Mary hugged her back.

She told her to come into the kitchen and she would put up a pot of coffee or tea. Ella told her that even though she loved coffee, it seemed that coffee didn't agree with her much anymore, so Mary made tea instead. "Milk and sugar?"

"No, just sugar," Ella replied. "Milk seems to take the taste of the tea away."

"That's how I drink it too." They both smiled.

Ella was a short woman with short, blonde hair. She must have been beautiful when she was young. She was beautiful now. They sat at the table gabbing. Then Mary heard the doorbell ring. It was the food. She excused herself for a short while until she paid the bill.

The man brought in all the food and drinks. It was quite heavy. He set it down on the counter in the kitchen. Mary paid the bill and gave him a handsome tip. "Thank you very much, lady."

She said, "You're welcome." She shut the door and asked Ella if she wanted some food to pick at until everyone got there, as she was already making up a plate for both of them.

Ella said, "I sure would. All I had today was a cup of tea. I was too excited, so I didn't eat."

"Neither did I," said Mary.

They both sat talking like old friends. She was quite a woman. Mary felt really comfortable talking to her. She told Mary that when she would pass by with her father, she would always tell him that Mary looked like a very nice person. Her father would agree.

"Well, thank you, Ella. You're very nice too. It's too bad I was so young. I really was very scared of Dad after all the things he said to my mom. I thought he knew she was very sick all the while and could not believe the treatment he gave her, knowing about that tumor."

"Your dad had no idea what was going on. He first heard about her death two weeks after she died. I believe he called you and wanted you to live with him."

"Yes, he did, but I felt horrible, thinking he deserted us in our hour of need. So I hung up. I have Alice and her husband coming to meet you today. They helped me out quite a bit and gave me room and board. They have loved me all my life and are childless, so they adopted me and treat me as their daughter. They happen to be wonderful people. I have been a very fortunate woman. Now you're added to the list. You're a great woman, Ella, and it's a pleasure getting to know you."

Everyone was coming in. All at once, the room filled up.

Mary started setting the table in the dining room. She introduced everyone to Ella. They got along famously. Ella had given Mary an envelope earlier, before anyone visited. Mary had put it in a drawer when she heard the man with the food. Then she got busy with all the guests. When she was going to bed, she opened it up. Her husband asked what she had. When she saw it, she could not believe what she was looking at.

"My dad left me millions in stocks and bonds, and Ella gave me a copy of her will. She's leaving me the house, her jewelry, and everything she owns."

"Wow," he said. "The stars are really in your corner this month, hon."

"They sure are, hon. This means we have no more worries about much anymore, and the kids can go to private schools. We might buy that boat we've always dreamt of too. My father was sure full of surprises, wasn't he?"

"He sure was, honey. This has been one eventful evening. Tomorrow we take all of this and go to a bank, and we have to look up a lawyer."

Mary said, "Dad took care of the lawyer. He wrote me a note about his best friend who has made him a very rich man." They had no idea how much they were worth. All they knew was they were very lucky people, with or without money. They kissed, put the light out, and made love. Then Frank went to sleep in Mary's arms.

They all went to Europe, including the cat. Ella was there, and so were Kevin and Alice. The kids loved Europe, and so did everyone else. They bought plenty of things and had them all shipped home. After the vacation, they all settled down a bit.

They were happy to be together. Once a week, they played poker. Usually, Kevin's friend Bob won. They had a lot of laughs, saying he cheated. They were a family that loved each other, so they were rich in more ways than one.

Through the years, they got closer. The women got along just terrifically, and the children loved the idea of having so many grandmothers. They got whatever they wanted.

In what seemed to be a very short time, the children grew up to be fine people. They were sent to the best schools, and both of them graduated with honors. Frank said they got their smarts from their mom. She said, "Yes, they did, but they got their looks from you, you handsome devil."

She kissed him. She said, "Life sure is funny, honey."

He said, "How is that?"

"Well, who would have thought that my dad would be rich someday and we would have such a wonderful life?"

"Well, I, for one, am sorry I never met him. I'm sure he saw you a thousand times. I'm told by Ella he passed this house each day to keep an eye out for us. He knew you were a sweetheart, or I never would have married you." He kissed her then.

They put the lights out and went to bed. They had had a very strenuous day, and both were tired. The kids yelled in from their rooms, "Will you two keep quiet? How are we going to get some sleep?" They laughed.